MANSON

MANSON

Christopher Pascale

VANTAGE PRESS
New York

Cover design by Polly McQuillen

FIRST EDITION

Published by Vantage Press, Inc.
419 Park Ave. South, New York, NY 10016

Manufactured in the United States of America
ISBN: 0-533-15160-0

Library of Congress Catalog Card No.: 2005900616

0 9 8 7 6 5 4 3 2 1

To Morton Trachtenberg

"Write like hell," he said.

MANSON

I

One foot in front of the other. Concentrate. Don't fall.

I made it to my table without falling. She was there.

"You're drunk again. Hank, you promised."

"I had one drink with an editor."

"Oh! Did he like your book? He must've liked it. I knew things would be getting better."

"Now, Harriet, let's not get ahead of ourselves, but I will tell you that he bought all the drinks. Did you order yet?"

"Not yet."

The waiter came over. He was tall and thin with dark hair greased to the side.

"Anything for you, sir?" he asked.

"Just a scotch, please."

"Anything to eat?"

"Oh, I . . ." she gave me a look, "of course. Just give me the lunch special. No salad or soup."

The food arrived with my third scotch. The special was shellfish over linguine. I'm allergic to shellfish. I got it wrapped to go and just drank my lunch. Harriet wasn't happy.

We were outside the restaurant.

"I have to get back to the office for a few hours. Deadlines and all." I started walking.

"Hank," she called, "take a cab."

"It's not far."

"But you've been drinking."

"I'll be fine. I'll call you when I finalize the next couple of chapters."

Made it back to my office. It was a dank little room with terrible illumination and no air conditioning. There was a little furnace on one of the walls that was never used. There were some roaches, but they never paid their share of the rent so I had to evict them myself. Truthfully, I always wrote at my apartment. I just came here to drink. I never believed that a writer should write in a small room with a typewriter. It's stupid. I took out a bottle of scotch and a glass. I started thinking.

There's a certain point you reach when you've been drinking where a certain sentiment takes over. I was feeling sorry for Harriet. She's just the kind of person who believed that things were going to get better. I'm a drunk, plain and simple. They were going to publish my book; I knew they would, the morons. I thought about calling her, but I didn't keep a phone there. I didn't want anyone calling if I actually decided to write, or drown myself in scotch and vomit and piss. I had recently written a sonnet about that. I usually wrote poems like that after having sex, especially after having sex with Harriet. I made love to her once. Afterwards, I went on a terrible binge that almost ended me. I spent three days straight (no food, no water, no alcohol) at a computer, and wrote *The Woman's Suicide*, by Henri Manson. Needless to say I haven't made love to her since. There's also a certain point you reach when you've been drinking where you get to forget the things you've let yourself remember.

I looked out the window. I drank through the night.

I stood up and started walking toward my apartment. While walking I looked at my hand. The glass was still there. I walked back into the office and put the glass down, and wrote myself a note to get more scotch. Then I passed out on my desk. The glass broke and the empty bottle fell to the floor.

While I was passed out, dehydrated with barely a pulse, Harriet was going to work. She was a university director of some sort. She helped foreign exchange students become accustomed to the country during their stay. Kind of like a guidance counselor. I think she can speak four languages.

I woke up at sunset. I thought it was only minutes later because the sky was just as dark as when I last looked, so I looked at the broken glass and fell back asleep. It was a deep, cold sleep.

While sleeping, drunk, I always became exposed to my self-conscious. I met it head on. I was expecting the typical dream where I would be driving down the street in a delivery truck. It would be a nice day, but no children would be outside, no cars would be on the road, and there was nothing for me to deliver. Seemed like a pretty good job. I was always happy during that dream. After the route was finished early, since there was nothing to deliver, I would pull up to a main road. There was a thirty second red light at the intersection during which I would tune out my thoughts and turn on the radio. The light turned green and, as I was rolling forward, the engine would stall and a Mack Truck would plow into me, launching me out the far side of my truck. I died on impact. It wasn't my fault.

But this dream was different. I was driving in a Volkswagen with a seven-year-old girl in the passenger seat. She had big blue eyes and brown hair down to her shoulders. 'Put on your seatbelt, Mister,' she said. I did. 'Can I get a book about maps at the store . . . and a globe, too?' she asked. 'Sure, I can get you those.' 'Promise?' She looked at

3

me all wide eyed with a smile absent one tooth. I smiled back at her. 'I promise.' We continued to drive. 'It's just over the toll bridge, sir. The rest of the world is over there.' 'What did you say?' I asked. 'That's the name of the store. It's the universal toy store.' We approached the booth. I threw exact change into the basket, and, with much assurance, drove toward the toy store.

'I can see it!' she said, 'I can see it! We're almost there, Mister.' 'I know. I can see it too.' And as those words were spoken I could feel my legs begin to stiffen and get heavy. After only a matter of seconds it became unbearable, and I had to stop as we pulled off the bridge. 'Are you okay, Mister? Mister, are you okay?' I had to walk for a little bit. I figured I had been driving for too long. 'Mister . . .' 'I'm . . . I'm okay. We'll be there in a second. Just . . . give me a second.' She waited patiently at first, and then she began to plead. I wanted to take her, but I couldn't move. The paralysis was unbearable. The sun began to set, she began to cry, and I eventually tuned her out as I looked at the rest of the world without thought of it rather than of myself, and she pointed toward it with tears in her eyes.

I woke up weak. My legs felt very light, as if they weren't there. I stood up, looked outside, and realized that I didn't know what day it was. My face felt tingly, and I wasn't sure whether I was hungry or tired. Half awake: I picked up the pieces of glass from the floor and left them on the desk.

I left the office. It was cold, dark, and empty outside. "Definitely has to be morning," I said to myself. I walked hurriedly toward my apartment I was half way there before I hailed a taxi to take me the rest of the way.

I walked into my apartment. The door was half open and the place was trashed. I was pretty sure I left it that way the last time I went out. Nothing seemed to be missing. Whatever.

I went into my refrigerator and took out a carton of milk and a box of stale cereal from the cupboard. "I gotta clean this place up." I took a bowl from the sink and rinsed it with cloudy faucet water. I bent my aching head over and rinsed the cottony texture from my mouth as well. As I picked my head up from the sink I noticed the clock reading four A.M. Sounded about right. I ate my cereal, and then watched the news until six when the phone rang.

"Hello?"

"Hank?" It was Harriet. "I'm sorry if I woke you."

"No you're not. You didn't though."

"I was wondering if you wouldn't mind helping me today."

"Depends on the time. I have work to do, and I just got back from the office two hours ago."

"Oh, did you finish the chapters?"

"There isn't a single word to show."

"You're too hard on yourself. Why don't you move in with me? You can relax." I was silent, not really listening. "Hank, are you there? Hank . . . ?"

"I'm here dammit!" I snapped. "I heard you!" There was a silence. I didn't want to be on the phone for another half hour over the whole process of making up. "I'm sorry, baby. I . . . I'm just so. . . ."

"I know. I shouldn't have brought it up. Why don't you get some sleep and tomorrow I'll come over and make you breakfast?"

"Yeah, alright, thanks. Tomorrow morning."

"Try to get some sleep."

We hung up.

I washed the dishes in the sink and took a short hot

shower, and a long cold one. I hadn't paid the utility companies in three months, but I guess they would prefer for one to suffer rather than grow mold. I appreciated that. After my shower I put on my torn brown robe. It was the only article of clothing that was clean. I peeled the clothes off my couch and my floor and my bed, and with my change jar I proceeded toward the laundry corridor. I knew the old man across the hall would give me a hard time, but I didn't really care.

As I turned the machine on I heard his door open behind me.

"Hey guy," said a young girl, "it's seven in the morning on a Saturday."

She had to have been sixteen. Her body was twenty-five. She had big brown eyes and beautiful, round mulatto cheeks, and short dark hair. This one would get me thrown in jail for the rest of my life.

"Did you hear me?" she asked.

"Yeah, I heard. Where's the old man that lived there?"

"Dunno," she said, "I moved in last week."

"My name's Hank, and this won't happen again."

"Good, because the contractors during the week are enough." She turned back toward her apartment. I was going to ask her name, but she turned back around. "Oh yeah," she said, "and don't stick that thing at me again. It's offensive." And she went inside.

I looked down and closed my robe.

I went back to my apartment and wrote three chapters and a series of letters and prose. They were awful: a direct result of nutrition, I felt. *'An artist has a hard time standing on his own because all he can work with is the scrapings of his beginning. As artists become more well known they become stronger because they can nurture their work as much as their body.'* That was from my failed thesis paper at

Bowdoin College. It's a member of the Little Ivy League. The professor told me that "a mockery of the arts is unacceptable, and philandering it as science will get you nowhere. I have no other choice, but to give you a zero, Mr. Manson. You can speak two languages. One of them has proven to be English. You knew the assignment."

Had he given me an extension I would have given him something I did not believe in its place, but he didn't. Ten percent was all I needed to pass. I didn't care about honors at that point, I felt desperate for a degree—I had promises to keep—and in such a case I was certainly willing to compromise. I wasn't prepared to sell out against four years of tuition on pride.

I wrote my mother a letter telling her I had graduated with honors—it was important to her that I excelled. She could not attend my graduation though; she moved back to France that year to take care of her sister who had cancer. I avoided contact with her for several months until I got a job that was expected of me—graduating with honors and all. In the meantime I was living with a friend from school, in Connecticut. His father got me a job bookkeeping on a farm. The farmer referred me to an advertising friend for an interview and told me all I really had to do was show up. Two days prior to my interview I heard news of my mother being murdered. An insane man threw her in front of a train. The funeral was held three weeks prior to my hearing of it. She had been dead for three weeks and I didn't even call. Not once. Not even to say hi and that I was doing well, to tell her that I was living with nice people.

I didn't attend my mother's funeral. I have yet to pay my respects. I never went to that interview, nor have I been to Connecticut since. I took the few hundred dollars I had and drove to Santa Monica, because it looked low class. In

Santa Monica I sold my car and moved into an apartment in the San Fernando Valley. That was ten years ago.

It was ten o'clock at night. I looked in the mirror; then I looked at my college photo. I looked like Hell. I felt empty and dead. With that, I fell asleep in front of a snow-screened television.

II

I woke up the next day to the sounds of Harriet in my kitchen. She was wearing a new dress, and she wore her long, dark hair down, and didn't blow-dry it straight. She was fairly tall for a woman, 5'8", and her body was curved and smooth.

Women always look best in their thirties. Men start to lose their hair and their charm. They forget how to laugh at themselves. I don't think I've laughed in years, or, at least, it feels that way.

I pretended to sleep while she cleaned the floor and the countertops. Then she came over to me.

"Hey," she said, "you fell asleep on the couch again. Cable's out."

"I know, I know. I've been waiting for you."

"I know. I felt your eyes on me while I was cleaning. Did you like it?"

"I like *you*. The dress is nice too."

"I bought it after we had lunch the other day."

"It's nice."

"I figured you'd appreciate it . . . in the morning at least."

"What?"

"You know you're always nicer after you've gotten some rest."

"That's because I usually have a hangover. In this case,

I just don't want you to leave . . . before I get something to eat, I mean."

"Well, before you start saying really nice things to me, why don't you sit down at the table before you fall asleep again?"

We walked toward the kitchen table. I sat down. She threw eggs and cheese into the frying pan, and poured me a glass of orange juice. Harriet did this every once in a while. She once told me that the only reason was so there would be food when she spent the night. She's just kind, and that's good, and it will be good when she's gone, too. I can foresee her going for good soon enough. Her sense of humor and sensual ways would be better appreciated elsewhere. I would tell her to leave now, but something compels me to make her stay for as long as she thinks I love her without me actually having to say it (maybe it's the breakfast). Shortly after she asks, she will leave. That is just the way it is. I do not feel it is something that I should lie about. It wouldn't have saved any of them for me to lie like that, so I just stopped making them die. Love is a component to death. [I didn't used to be like this.] When a loved one goes, we do as well, but we can never do quite as well, and that is where most people are surprised. There is no triumph from losses, only the tribulations that come with them. And that is okay. All of these things are part of our small existence.

I finished the omelet.

"Let us go for a walk. It is nice outside. You can bring your notebook and your pen, and we'll go to one of those benches along the walking path."

"We can. I don't know if I have much in me. I finalized some chapters last night."

"You wrote?"

"In between sleeping."

10

"That figures. Only you would write a book in your sleep."

"Let's go while it's still early."

We went to the path; it was shaded by trees for the most part, but the light still bothered my eyes. It was the closest to the country I cared to be. There was a river, a stream really, that ran along it, and across from the water, on the other side of the path, were trees. Every quarter mile, or so, there was a bench, and every half mile there was a drinking fountain. We walked a mile. During our walk I noticed all the birds that were around and the sounds that the squirrels made while hiding acorns in the bushes when they didn't think anyone could see them. I just sat there on a bench in the park for forty-five minutes writing an essay about how people limit the life of fictional characters to what they get to see of them. They act as though there was nothing other than what they know, or get to know. But I realized most people treat real people like that too, and although I finished the essay, and it would probably make its way into *The Review*, all I could feel was the hostility that came with the judgment I held for the strangers that were jogging and picnicking; when I didn't even know how they got there in the first place.

I suppose that was sad. I didn't feel sad.

III

It was Sunday morning. The sky was dark and the air was cold. I expected it to warm up after the clouds passed. They didn't, so I stayed in bed until noon. At that time I rolled out of bed and got a bottle of scotch and a glass. With the glass and bottle I brought an old book to bed (*Love is a Dog From Hell,* by Charles Bukowski) and sat back with my short glass of scotch. After a few poems I put it down. *Numb your ass, your heart, and your brain.* What the hell does he know?

I continued to drink, and while I drank a great many poems went through my head, but I refused to write them down. I believed that an artist shouldn't write while under any influence; be it drugs or insanity, because they don't expand the mind. They narrow the thoughts so much that the creation is narrow itself; causing its creator to become dependent on those substances in order to finish, to maintain consistency.

At three o'clock I got out of bed. The sky was still overcast and it began to rain, but a little rain is okay, too. My eyes remained transfixed on the yellow walls across the way while I stared into the space between it as the water fell upon the dusty walkway. It was the first rain I'd seen in months. When I rose from my stupor, minutes later, I saw the girl from the other day running out into the courtyard in shorts and a tee shirt, without a care in the world. When she reached the middle she did a cartwheel and laid down, looking at the darkened sky. My phone rang ten minutes into the show while the rain just kept falling onto the earth, and her, and shut my door. She wasn't there next time I checked. I guess she figured she had been there long enough. The call was from an editor. That figured.

"Hello."

"Mr. Manson? Hi, my name is Juliet Winters. Robert assigned me to your book." Robert Cambden was the editor I met with a few days before, prior to my lunch with Harriet. "I was calling to see if you had anything for me to look at."

As she finished her sentence the glass dropped from my hand and broke.

"Balls!"

"I'm sorry?"

"What? Oh, no. Not you." I said. "Not my . . . uh . . . I . . . I finalized some chapters. You can see them if you like."

"Alright," she said. She sounded a bit confused. "Do you think it would be possible to bring them in today?"

"Well, we can meet somewhere and discuss them."

"That shouldn't be necessary. You can bring them by my office," she said.

I didn't care what she wanted to do so I agreed and told her to expect me within the hour. With some reluctance she added that she was looking forward to meeting me. An hour-and-a-half later I brought the pages to her office, but left them with her secretary. She didn't need me there anyway.

As I was walking away from the building I kept thinking about what Cambden could have been thinking when he assigned the Winters girl to me. Or was I assigned to her? It didn't really matter, I suppose. She just sounded so arrogant. I could picture her in her office in her expensive chair, and across from her brand new desk, which was beautifully coordinated with the walls, was her degree framed on one of those walls, and next to that would soon be her MBA in literature or journalism. What was that "Juliet" and "Mr. Manson" stuff? I haven't won the Nobel Prize or a Pulitzer. She had to have been new. It was the only acceptable explanation for all the formalities.

Eventually I got over myself and decided that she was just being polite.

My usual day continued. It was seven in the evening. As it became later I was more drawn to go outside, but usually didn't. I made a point of abandoning shelter only at times of sunset and sunrise. In most cases I was passed out or too drunk to leave. I looked out my front door at the yellow walls, noticing the orange and purple sky as the sun tucked itself in. I shut the door and drank glass after glass of the cloudy water from my faucet until I began to sweat. After I went to the bathroom I continued to drink more glasses of water while the snow-screened television kept me company. At eight o'clock I filled a glass with orange juice, toasted a few slices of bread and spread strawberry jam across them.

After eating, I rushed to the library before it closed and stole a package of lined paper after taking out *Timequake*, by Kurt Vonnegut. While I was at Bowdoin I took a special interest in his short stories, and read all of his books except for this one. I didn't even know he wrote another book. I rushed home sweating, and in a bit of a panic. I quickly relieved myself in the bathroom when I returned. I was always nervous whenever I did something stupid, like stealing paper from the library or band-aids from the doctor's office.

My apartment was dark. It was dark, but the streetlights poured into my bedroom window. I opened *Timequake* and read the inside cover. I noticed that I had not read the book he wrote before this, *Fates Worse Than Death*. I decided I would read it next. Having free time offers people a few luxuries they seldom appreciate. I never felt pressed to read fast, which was good since I couldn't, nor did I cloud my mind much. I think the latter came from not really caring about anything, which stemmed from my belief that I didn't feel I knew anything. I read the first hundred pages, laughed my ass off through half of them, and then fell asleep for a few hours.

I woke to a loud crash outside my bedroom. I stayed in bed. There was nothing to steal from me anyway, and besides, getting stabbed or beat up otherwise really sucks. I could feel someone at my door. I pretended to be sleeping. I felt my pulse tapping on the inside of my neck as I heard the footsteps getting closer. I did my best to remain calm, then, sliding across my arm, I could feel a hand. It was a man's hand. I quivered in fear and was sweating coldly, and the hand was over my shoulder; I felt it on my neck; foreign and rough. Then the hand held itself tightly over my mouth. I jerked my body upward and screamed. I grabbed for the hand, but there was none. I looked around, but saw no one. I sat up the rest of the night afraid to move. I didn't read or write or drink. I just sat still in my bed with my back against the wall until the sun came up. Imagine that, a grown man afraid of his own shadow.

I got out of bed to the sound of mail in my door slot. It was an uncommon sound. I picked up a literary magazine with a check attached for $38. It was for a poem I sent in months ago. They pay $2 per line.

Confrontation
By: Jonathan Henri

She threw me a line from the dock.
Saved my life,
now she owes me.

Lately it feels more as though
she owns me.

"It is time to go," I tell her,
but you know how women are.

"Do you not love me?" she asks.

I answered not.
I owed her nothing.
She, at the very least,
could have offered me silence.

How could I love one
who looks at me so strangely
intrigued while never understanding
that there is nothing wrong with
standing on fives and fours?
And how can I care for how one feels
when she is always keeping score?

Jonathan Henri was the name I used when I sent poetry to anthologies and magazines figuring that they might
assume that I held some relationship to the late American
regionalist painter, Robert Henri. I wrote that poem when
Harriet and I first became involved. I felt intimidated, I
suppose. It was always a nice surprise to see my name in

some magazine. I always act as though I don't care, but there is no greater aphrodisiac for me than that. I once told myself that if I ever became homeless it couldn't last for more than a year, because my name wouldn't be in the phonebook anymore.

I thought of how I'd have to be careful of myself when the book came out and the publisher signed a five-figure check to my name. I didn't worry about it much, though. I figured I'd be dead by then. Thinking about it suddenly sent a chill into me. I never really cared before, but it felt as though the score really was being kept.

IV

I met with Juliet Winters later that day to discuss the chapters. We ordered lunch at an outdoor restaurant near the publishing office. I ordered mineral water and a plate of pasta. She had a bottle of red wine and a small salad. She talked after we ate.

"I read the chapters, Mr. Manson. I was very impressed, but for the sake of the public, perhaps we can add a few apiaries. What do you think?"

"I don't think so, Miss Winters."

"But people like memorable things that they can cleverly add into conversation. Like John Donne when he said . . ." she did finish her sentence, but I wish she had never started it.

I realized what I was dealing with.

"Aside from the fact that an apiary is a collection of beehives," I began, trying not to sound too sarcastic. "I do not feel any *aphorisms* should be added. I wrote a memorable story, half on the side of slavery, sure, but memorable no less. I don't want to be some quote, furthermore detaching myself from any world that might be real. Do you know anything about John Donne other than the fact that he wasn't a Florida Key?"

She stared at me blankly. I felt like apologizing, but realized that it was just the silence. Space makes most people uncomfortable, causes them to do things they wouldn't do under other circumstances. I looked at her watch from across the table and concluded our meeting. "Look at the time. I'm sorry, but I have a friend to meet. Will you excuse me?"

"Yes," she said, "and please feel free to bring me anything you have finished within the next couple of days."

"Will do. Have a nice day."

She stood up to shake my hand and I almost apologized again. I admit I was intimidated by her prior to that engagement, and that the only reason I agreed to meet her was because I was hungry, but I looked forward to handing her a few more chapters. She looked very pretty when she was being insulted. I suppose she was about twenty-three. She had no real shape to her body and she wasn't very sexy. Sexy comes from smart. She did, though, have very soft looking red hair and hazel eyes. Her lips were pouty, like those of a child's, and she had freckles on her nose.

I got back to my apartment, wrote half a chapter, and gave $20 to my landlord for a little hot water and some good faith. Juliet probably went back to her office and then to her nice suburban neighborhood. She must've slept well because skin and hair that nice never came from working hard or stressing over the rent, or deciding which day you were going to eat.

I turned on my snow-screened television when the phone rang.

"Hello?"

"Hank? Hi."

"Hi, Harriet. What d'you want?"

"What? Nothing. I'm just calling to see how you are, that's all."

"Fine."

"Fine is good. Maybe you can drone a little more, though." There was a silence. But she was right in what she said. "I was thinking about you at work today. I swear, I almost jumped a man in the street when his footsteps sounded like yours."

"Why didn't you?"

"Turned out to be a broad-shouldered woman wearing men's shoes."

"Otherwise you would have?"

"Oh, I see. You want to play that game. Okay, tell me how your meeting was with your supposed editor, Juliet."

"We both know the answer to that."

"Yeah, we know, but give me a verb."

"She sucked."

"Generous woman."

"I meant that she was awful."

"Well, you'll have to try again until she gets it right, I guess."

"I guess so."

"Well, enough of that for now," she said. "You know, I think we're gonna be alright."

I then remembered that I had to pick up a bottle of scotch for the office.

"If I get my work done," I said.

"You will. Can I see you tonight? I have a conference, but I was thinking that I could take you out afterward."

"I was planning on going to the office tonight. Deadlines and all."

"No problem. Just an idea. I have to go now. I'll just stop by in a couple of days."

"Alright, how about two?"

She agreed.

I walked toward the office at ten, not really feeling as though I had the strength in me to drink through the night.

I figured I was getting old. I picked up a bottle of cheap scotch on the way.

At the office I took off my shirt and went to lay myself across the desk, but saw the glass I left from the week before. I pushed the glass off the desk to the floor, where I suppose I should've left it, because the dust remained where I wanted to lay, and all of the broken pieces broke into smaller ones. I shrugged my shoulders and laid my back on the desk. I was just lying there staring up at the broken ceiling fan. Then I looked at the clogged ventilation duct in the wall. I probably could've sued the guy that rented me the place. Whatever. I opened the bottle. I didn't have a glass so I just stared at the ceiling fan and fell asleep.

In my sleep I found myself walking on clouds, skipping across the air. I felt a light sensation over my body better than the effects of any numbing drug. I looked up and saw unicorns flying over me. They were shaded with pretty purple, pink and green pigments, and as they all passed over me I looked at my feet, which were winged. Then, offering proof of gravity, all of the unicorns began defecating on me, ten pounds at a time, which were twenty-two Newtons of force, meaning that I, floating, exerted twenty-two Newtons of force toward them. Funny how I would apply physics to a situation while I was wiping corn out of my eyes. Since when do unicorns eat corn anyway? And what's the deal with corn and a person's body? It's not synthetically sweetened.

An old man that looked like Gandhi approached me and put his hand on my shoulder. "They always get you when you least expect it," he said. Then he walked away. The back of his shirt was covered with turd stains. I hate being sober.

I woke up with a terribly rough feeling in my throat and nose. I lifted the small bottle viciously and poured the whole thing over my face. Maybe half of it went in my mouth. What I could swallow went down like nails, and caused a rampage in my stomach. I lay back regretfully, and sat in my chair.

All of a sudden I was in shock. I saw blurry lights fly past me as I was being moved. I tried to focus, but all I could see were translucent faces over me as the table underneath me was being wheeled down a corridor with a brown ceiling. I figured I was done. This was it, and I was too weak to fight it. *Come on and get me you bastards. Come on and get me*, I thought. *You knew when to come, and now all you have to do is finish what I started.*

I was suddenly alone. I felt my eyesight regain itself, but there was nothing. Then I felt the table turn over, and as I was released from it I began falling toward a sea of fire until the chains at my wrists and ankles snapped tight. And I hung, my limbs stretched, to die for a life of error. The greatest one being that I thought I could try. And demonic laughs and wails came from all sides of me as the fire rose up. I tried to tune it out, go to another place, but as I closed my eyes my lashes and brows fell to dust, then the lids melted off of my eyes, and the skin on my face was charred. The demonic laughs grew more voluminously causing their presence to be overwhelming. I shook as hard as I could, trying to break from the chains in order to be merciful to myself, but I could not. I felt my joints stretch as the flames encompassed my body for seconds at a time until I eventually gave in; realizing that there was no mercy for the weak and the pained, only contemptuous slander, and there never would be. I just hung there dead, until I too was released with all of the other guilty people. And as I fell into the endless pit of ash I was eventually eased into a halt where my motionless, unfeeling body would lay.

In the midst of it all I soon came to realize what the great poet meant when she spoke of ashes from cinders . . . that it never really meant anything anyway. How there was heat from false conviction and bribery of the dead. When we are gone, we are gone all the same despite the hatred and the love we held. We are gone. How robust one can be, how meek we all are. We are gone. We will join them and we will be gone. We will be gone all the same.

I woke up on the floor kicking my desk in a frenzy; cold, sweating. I felt for my face finding my eyebrows and my eyelashes. And the silence, absent of the demonic sounds, was painful. I laid on the floor, thinking. I hated my life; I hated my life. I didn't think of whom I should blame, but I began to think of my mother dying at the hands of a madman. Then I thought about Harriet dying at her own hand, aided by my demeanor. I walked back to my apartment. On my way in I noticed the new girl sunbathing in the middle of the grassy courtyard. It was likely to be a good summer. I never saw the grass so green. I was thinking she was Haitian. I toyed with thoughts of her being from the Galapagos Islands, but dismissed it, realizing that she would not be here after living in a paradise.

I went to a new notebook and began writing letters and prose again. Soon, with a cold hand, I took on a madman's authorship, which is what I refer to when I think of an artist placing himself within the work, delivering rhythm from his subconscious. That kind of work has been said to be the best at times. Rarely has it ever been outlawed, reason not being for its great value, but because it was not found to be offensive toward Anglo housewives and husbands in the mid-western United States.

When I was finished I had written just over sixty pages, composing eight poems. The longest one finished off the series in thirty-five. I later burned them outside in the courtyard, and as I watched the pages burn I realized that nothing would change. Ashing the paper still left the words to be true, and before me, standing across the fire, was my mother in a long dress, and she was approaching me. The flames caught her dress and she began to burn. I took off my shirt and tried to tackle her in order to smother the fire, but I somehow jumped through her. She stood, silently, looking at me with sincere eyes. She eventually burned to the ground and the wind swept away her ashes as well as the pages that I burned. I began to feel the sky climb upon me, and my body felt terribly heavy, forcing me to lay myself down and close my eyes. I accepted the blame. It was easiest that way. The truth usually is.

V

I awoke at nighttime, disoriented. I walked around my apartment for twenty minutes before any conscious thoughts entered my mind. I decided to sit down and write. I fell back into my sleep, in a chair, only to wake up through the night.

It was ten A.M. eventually, and I filled a dirty glass from the sink with orange juice and toasted some bread while I looked at the pages on the table, forgetting when it was that I last wrote. They were good. I ate the toast and drank the orange juice and gave Juliet a call telling her to expect me in an hour or so. She asked me to meet her later in the evening at a café where Cambden wanted to meet. I agreed.

I left my place at about five. I looked at the window of the café. *One of these,* I thought as I walked in. It wasn't such a bad place, but all of these cafés, being so popular, have made a cup of coffee $6, and even a glass of water costs money. Cambden wasn't there, but I saw Juliet at a table. She stood to greet me, but more so to show off her brand name dress. It was a short, black velour deal. I shook her hand and offered common courtesy as I would any woman posing as a lady.

Cambden was caught at an editor's meeting I was told. Funny that she, an editor, was not there as well.

"Do you have the pages?" she asked.

"Yeah, right here." I gave them to her.

"I'll read them later. You know, I wanted to mention

what a pleasure it is to work with you. Some of the other writers I've worked with are just so . . ." she was making some sort of a gesture with her hand, ". . . you know?"

"Did you make any changes?" I asked.

"None. Mr. Cambden was very pleased with them as well. He wanted me to give you this." It was a watch. "It's a *Cartier*," she added.

I accepted it and asked her to thank him for me. A waiter came over.

"May we have a bottle from the Rose Garden Vineyards? Red, please. Is wine alright with you, hon?"

Hon? She called me "hon." Whatever.

"Yeah, fine," I said.

"Oh," she said, "the player is back."

A piano player went to the corner where he was hiding during his performance. I couldn't make out his face, but he was small, and I mean small all over. He was short and his shoulders were narrow with a hunched posture when he wasn't sitting on his bench. On the bench, however, he appeared somewhat tall.

"Usually," she continued, "he plays classical music, but last week he played jazz. It was wild."

"I'm sure it was."

"Do you like the classics, Hank?"

"I don't mind them, but I don't really listen to much music."

The waiter came over with a bottle of red.

"From the Rose Garden Vineyards, '83," he said. Juliet looked delighted.

"Do you have anything from 1982, perhaps?" I asked. "Maybe something French?"

"Oh, Hank," Juliet said, "everything French is so overrated. This will be fine."

The waiter poured the wine into our glasses and then placed the bottle down.

"Are you hungry, Hank?"

"Not really."

She turned to the waiter.

"This will be fine, thank you. Oh, I'm sorry, may I have a soufflé?"

"Of course, madam."

She dismissed him with a nod. She leaned toward me with an elbow on the table and her fingers were twirling in her hair. She talked about herself for the most part, overemphasizing the movements of her mouth. When she drank she placed her lips repeatedly on the same place, when she tilted her glass. I figured she had spent too much time with stupid men. Eventually she grew tired of me not noticing how sexy she was. The piano, a pleasant consolation, however, sounded very nice in the background. He played for about forty-five minutes before taking a break. We finished the wine. The waiter delivered Juliette's soufflé and then asked if we would care for anything else.

"Another bottle would suit us very well."

"Wait," I said, "I'll have a glass of water, and bring the lady a single glass rather than a bottle. Nothing from '83."

"Oh, Hank," she said waving her hand at me. She looked at the waiter. "That will be fine." He left as she dismissed him.

Juliet continued to lean forward as she spoke to me. I continued to offer disinterested body language. It only seemed to entice her more.

The player was back.

"What is this song?" I asked.

"The *Moonlight Sonata,* by Beethoven."

She continued to speak, but I listened to the player instead. The continuous rhythm was maddening. I lost myself within the bars and phrases while she spoke her speak, and the keys continued to touch upon their strings. It was genius. The piece was so simple, and I suppose that in those moments I was a prisoner to its simplicity.

"So tell me about your place, Hank. I'm sure you've been terribly bored with me talking this whole time." She continued for another minute or so. Her speech was beginning to slur and her dress was practically in my pocket. I finished my water and excused myself to the men's room. Meanwhile she had taken care of the check.

We walked out of the café.

"Do you want to see my place?" she asked.

"I'm afraid it's a bit too far for it being this time of night." I then realized that it was half past six in the evening. She caught the hint, though. I was merely maintaining my boundaries of professionalism, sure. When I got back to my apartment it was seven o'clock. I figured I'd just write a little and hope to pass by the new girl as I went through the laundry corridor. I didn't see her.

I went to my apartment thinking how stupid Juliet was. What was Cambden thinking? She would end me. I had to call Harriet. I needed to hear her voice. Her phone rang. I got her machine. I hung up. After three hang ups I left a message asking her to call me back.

I stood in the middle of my apartment and it all went before me in a flash. I stood, like some harlequin, in the midday at a circus and there was this woman with blood coming out of her head, flowing like strands of hair. She gave me assistance in my role of immortality, as all harlequins are immortal. And with that thought the sounds of the ocean were in my head moving about as I prepared to die within life one more time. It was like hearing the *Moonlight Sonata* sober, wishing I was drunk so I didn't have to appreciate it. Then I recalled when it all began as I flashed to the instant of Harriet killing herself that night. And I thought of how I was dying, and how it didn't seem so bad.

The phone rang.

"Hello?"

"Hi, Hank, I got your message. Are you okay?"

"What?"

"I got your message. You said to call as soon as I got in. Are you okay?"

"Oh, Harriet. Yeah, I'm fine. I guess I just fell asleep for a little while. Can you come over?"

"Why don't you go back to sleep and I'll see you tomorrow?"

"Why not now?"

"Because I have no money for cab fare and you'll be passed out when I get there."

We hung up the phone.

I woke up mentally when I heard the front door open. I heard her footsteps approach my bed, but they sounded heavy, which was odd. She stopped near me. I could smell her.

She slowly dragged the tips of her fingernails along my ankles to my thighs. I then felt them along my side and goose bumps covered my entire body as she reached my neck. Then she slid her open palm down my body and blew her sweet breath gently against my face and neck. I looked up at her. She was right. I did appreciate her more in the morning. And then she jumped on me with her curly black hair all jostled, and her big soft lips smothered mine. Who needs foreplay anyway?

After a couple of minutes I rolled out of bed and got her a bottle of water from her bag, and cleaned myself up with a washcloth. I guess I could've used some foreplay. It was an old one anyway. We slept for an hour and held each other for another.

I rolled out of bed at about ten o'clock and cooked some eggs and toast, and filled a clean glass with orange juice.

Later in the day Harriet took me to get a haircut and the publishing company gave me $1,000. We bought a pair of shoes, a couple of pairs of pants, and some shirts. Then I paid my landlord for the next month's rent and four months use of utilities. He looked at me funny, as if he was insulted. Then I took Harriet out to dinner and we spent the night at her place. I broke out a new one, and, again taught myself why foreplay is important.

VI

"On the rack!" a voice called. It was a woman's voice, cold and shrill. Two men grabbed me and strapped me to a table, and then the voice's face approached. She had wild blonde hair and a fair complexion. Her long fingernails were lightly crossing upon my cheek. "You know you are deserving of this," she said.

"Well," I said, "I believe in self-denial, personally."

"Is that so? Strange creature," she said. "Follow my eyes. I want you to watch me do it."

I followed them. Her eyes left, and she laughed as they did. They were replaced by those of a man's. He was tall and very broad. The table I was strapped to was turning toward the floor and it began to separate in the middle. I felt my spine begin to tear and my body was breaking. The floor began to spin and then I was forced to face the man's eyes again. They were black and hollow, captivating. They forced mine open. I lost all thoughts following the still disposition they held. Then, he waved his hand over my face. A voice called from the distance; a cold, shrill voice. It hurt from my neck to my heels to hear it. I tried to do away with the thoughts I held—they pained me much—but I did not really believe in self-denial. Excuses ought to be saved for other people's regularities. I always felt that living with oneself was denial enough.

The hand was still over my face and I eventually surrendered to the truth of it all. I closed my eyes and simply accepted what was to be. I had chances. I made decisions. Now, as it would have been for anyone else, it was time to pay my dues. It was probably just a big scam anyway. I'll get recycled—given my failure—and I will know one more thing, at least, when I return.

All of my pages were at the publisher's office waiting to be printed. Juliet set up a reading at a museum in Los Angeles and signings at some of the smaller bookstores in the county. Cambden, being polite, kept me posted about the marketing scheme, but he also assumed that I had little clue as to what he was talking about. I felt that they were overpricing it, but the publishers said that the manuscript was test marketed by several hundred housewives over the last two weeks and that the reviews were phenomenal. Some of them wrote personal statements on how they connected in relation to Colette, the story's tragic heroine. None were negative. They offered me a small commission in addition to the original contract. We settled on a bonus and a short-term travel account based on the event that the book was a best seller.

During the time between the book coming out and my rent running out Juliet took me out to lunch a lot. She called with a new excuse every day. Either she had a friend who wanted to meet me, or some new idea for promoting the book. She wanted me to get involved in the Los Angeles nightlife. Whenever she spoke I heard water flowing all around me. Eventually I used it to tune her out, allowing me to enjoy the free lunch.

Two days prior to the reading in L.A., Juliet left early to get acquainted with the people there. She called it networking. Cambden told me that she was probably getting coked out of her head. I found out that my book was the first she successfully completed in the sixteen months she'd been with the firm, and that the reason she was still with the company was because her father owned the press. I just assumed that she was inarticulate, but she wasn't that fortunate.

I arrived at the museum the following day. "Christ!" I said to myself, "everything gets killed here." The museum was in the typical Renaissance style disgraced by a Gothic façade.

I went into the museum. Juliet was the first to greet me. She was wearing a short dress and she changed her hair. It was short and loose about her jaw, dyed mousy brown.

"Darling, hi," She kissed me on both my cheeks. "We've been expecting you."

Behind her, smoking large cigars and drinking champagne, were four men. Their names were all probably Rolph or Theodore.

"I love these clothes," Juliet went on, "this new style of yours is outrageous. These are the men who set up your reading."

"I'm impressed," I said. Of course, it was that it only took four of them to arrange a time to tell the janitor to put fifty chairs in the lobby, but they were pleased that I was impressed and offered me a glass of champagne.

We all drank champagne and they smoked their large cigars. They discussed trends and apartments. I excused myself momentarily and walked around the museum. I appreciated the silence. I was accustomed to being alone. I recognized the pieces from the false Pollock collection. It was one of those paintings done by a monkey on a tricycle, dripping paint on the canvas. I began to think of Juliet and the men she was drinking with; how they spoke of parties and celebrity status. Then I thought about my clothes and the stupid glass I was drinking from; how I used to keep a snow-screened television on in my apartment because it was comfortable, like a friend without the ardor, or any of the other things that got in the way when it came to relationships. I placed the glass on a marble stone top and walked back to the museum group.

"Oh, the artist," one of them stated upon my return.

"Tell us about your work. We do love art."

"I'm sorry," I said, "but I have a friend to meet and I'm already late."

I left. I was expecting Juliet, or one of the men, to snap her fingers to call for a black man in a white suit to open the front door for me, but that didn't happen. It seemed to be like that everywhere else in the city.

I hailed a cab, and went back to the hotel. I called Harriet.

"Hey," I said.

"Hey yourself. How's LA?"

"It's alright. Are you sure you can't come here for the reading?"

"I really can't. I'm sorry, but I promise that I'll go to the signing when you get back. You should go out tonight and use that publisher's account while you can."

"I don't know. I think I'll just order some room service."

"Do what you want. I have to go though. Work and all."

"Alright," I said, "I'll see you in two days." We hung up.

I looked around the hotel room. It was half the size of my apartment, but nicer. There was a small balcony that overlooked the pool. I was on the fifth floor. The little refrigerator with overpriced liquor and candy was half empty. They'd probably charge me for that. There was a basket on the bed, courtesy of Cambden and Juliet's father. It had a bottle of mineral water, macadamia nuts and Belgium truffles. Juliet must have told them that I don't drink. I would think that Cambden should have known better if he really had anything to do with sending me a basket.

The bed was firm and comfortable. I laid back with the pillows propped up while I ate the chocolates and drank the water while watching television. There was nothing good on so I looked at the movies I could order; only cheap sex movies. I had no problem with cheap sex movies, but I felt funny about ordering them under the publisher's bill. I continued to flip through the channels. I finished the chocolates—sixty of them—drank the mineral water and ate most of the macadamia nuts. After the nuts I went to the fridge and drank three four-dollar sodas. After finishing the last one it was midnight and I was ready to climb the walls. I needed to occupy myself.

I took a glass from the nightstand and listened in on the people next door. They were two men, and I was pretty sure they were the stylish young men who checked in at the same time I did. They were grad students at Stanford. They brought it up *casually* while standing on line. They were both probably going to be lawyers or accountants. You could tell. There was just something about them that no one could like. While I was listening I heard one fussing about his hair while the other was looking for his cellular phone. They were leaving soon. I put on my shirt, my pants, and my shoes, and walked behind them. While one of them was putting his plastic slide key in his wallet I acted as though I was passing them and purposely tripped over his foot. He fell too. While picking myself up I put one of my keys on the ground and picked his up.

"I'm terribly sorry young man. Are you alright?" I asked.

"Hey, you have to watch it, jerk," the other said. His friend agreed.

"Gee, I said I'm sorry. What d'ya say I buy you a drink and we'll call it even? Both of you."

After being reprimanded by them I decided that no actions were too cruel for these boys, and that there was no sense in letting a couple of idiots spoil a perfectly good sugar rush. They went their own way. I went to my room letting them think they won. Then I went to theirs.

Their room was the same as mine, only with two beds. I found one of their credit cards, picked up the phone and ordered enough gay male porn to last through the morning. Then I raided their whole snack bar and stacked mine full. I ate what was left, all candy and chips. I fell asleep at three. The reading was in nine hours.

I woke up continually through the night with stomach pains. All of the antacids in the world couldn't have helped me. I waited it out. I got out of bed at nine in the morning and sat in a whirlpool bath to relieve the tension in my back and bowels. It worked rather quickly and I jumped out of the tub, relieved myself fully, took a shower, you know . . . to clean it all out, and went back into the bathtub. It was quite nice actually.

I dressed in a plain cotton shirt and a pair of chinos. It was too sunny out to wear dark clothes, and shorts would have been inappropriate to wear to a reading. I walked down into the lobby. The college boys were checking out and looked awfully perturbed.

"I am sorry sir," said a woman from behind the counter, "but I did not see you leave last night and you did not leave your key here at the front desk." I approached. She continued. "I have to charge an additional $60 to your bill for the key, $200 for the snack bar, and we charge $6 for every rental. Is this your credit card number?" she asked.

"Look," he said defensively, "I did not order *any* movies or eat from the snack bar. I was *out* all night."

"Then who did?" she asked. "Did someone else go into your room, eat your refrigerator empty, and then order *Jailhouse Rocketships* parts one through six on *your* credit card? I cannot allow special privileges."

I smiled with self-gratification prior to intervening.

"Excuse me . . ." I paused to look at her nametag, "Alice. I couldn't help but overhear this minor discrepancy. Perhaps this will help." I took the key out of my pocket and put it on the counter. "I found this outside of my room before I turned in last night. I was going to give it to its owner when I found it, but I heard some noises from the room, so, needless to impart, I chose to wait."

He looked at me. He knew. To hell with him.

"Well," I said, "I must be going. Schedules and all."

I put on my sunglasses and left. The boy and his tall friend were speechless, and I felt good all the way to the museum.

"There you are, sweetie," Juliet announced in a high voice. "I was worried you were going to be late."

"I decided to walk. It's a nice day." I looked at my watch. "I still have half an hour."

Juliet reintroduced me to the museum guys from the other day and I met a few of the critics. They all told me how much they loved art, as though they were trying to convince themselves, and how much they were looking forward to hearing my work. They were mostly movie critics, and art critics, and book critics all from the Los Angeles area. It was considered chic to serve wine from the Rose Garden Vineyards at affairs in LA, I was told while being offered a glass. I waved the waiter away and asked for a club soda. A woman ten feet away asked a man to get her a club soda as well. Minutes later I heard the same woman call the waiter an idiot, exclaiming that she did not order seltzer, and how he was to blame for her dress being ruined, since she spilled it on herself.

Juliet approached me with a copy of my book. It was an 8″ by 5″ hardcover. **MANSON** was written on the side, all in capital letters. Meanwhile, the sound was being tested at the podium. A speaker representing the museum began. Everyone offered their attention and sat upon request as I was called to read.

I walked up to the podium and looked at thirty-five pairs of disinterested eyes, each measuring me up the same as a pig in question of slaughter. I focused on points over their heads and began. I didn't tell them the truth of how I came to write the book. Rather, I told them that my style stemmed from observing the world around me, a skill I gained in college, and from my observations I had been able to create a narrator separate from myself, allowing my work to become impersonal. I should have told them that I perfected my craft writing movie scripts. At least they would have been remotely interested. So I read.

I read for twenty minutes: enough to get into the story without boring everyone to death. When I finished the museum speaker thanked me and took a picture with Juliet and me. Apparently, Juliet was my manager. The critics stayed as long as the wine, and then they were gone as well. I stayed and looked at the paintings for a while. I always appreciated portrait paintings because all they really were were family pictures equivalent to today's photographs. Now, they're priceless. That is, of course, until a price is offered. I left the museum at three and ate a deli sandwich while strolling through a city park. It was nice to get to a place where everything seemed simpler in a city so pretentiously laid back.

VII

I went back to my hotel room around sunset and thought about going out. I figured I was leaving in the morning and I had not seen this place at night; I found little reason to return. The phone rang. It was the front desk telling me that Harriet was on the line.

"Hank, hi."

"Hi."

"How was the reading?"

"It went well. It's . . . it's nice to hear from you."

"Well I missed you, and I have some good news."

"Met the man of your dreams?"

She ignored my comment, probably figuring that I had been drinking.

"Now, I don't know if you'd be interested in this, but the president of the university heard about you and would like to speak to you about a position on the faculty. What do you think?"

"What do you mean he '*heard* about me?' " I asked in an accusing tone.

"Look," she said, "don't be an asshole. You can just say no."

"What would make you even think that that would even interest me? What, are you trying to keep me close to you while I still suck and nobody knows me?"

"I was only giving you a suggestion." I could hear the

frustration in her voice. She didn't cry, though. "Why don't you just go? I'm sorry I called."

She hung up the phone. I turned on the shower, but realized that I couldn't leave it at that. I mean I believe that we all have a right to kill ourselves, but this kind of ending would break my rhythm, only leaving me vulnerable in later encounters. Worse yet, I'd probably wind up with Juliet. I called Harriet back. I got her machine and left a message. I called again five minutes later and she answered.

We talked for an hour then I sat in the shower and decided to take a whirlpool bath when I got the idea for my next book. I wrote a little of it in my head and then jumped out of the tub and ordered room service. I began writing on a hotel pad about an author who got a really great deal that allowed him to charge any item he considered essential to his craft to his publisher's account, which included the penthouse he moved into, the food he ate, and Mont Blanc pens that he could only use to write on paper that was made in a small eighteenth-century paper mill in Eastern Europe, which, of course, the publisher paid for. I went on about how he would spend his evenings alone in his solarium drinking brandy and eating mangos while sitting in a fine leather chair as his large boa knife sat in its buckskin case on a small side table constructed of English oak. The knife was essential for peeling mangos and grapefruits, and the table was essential for holding his knife. Then I went on about how his nights consisted of smoking a foot long Cuban cigar on his balcony as he watched the airplanes touch down on the runway of the San Diego Airport. He would only come into contact with the people who did his laundry and delivered his groceries. He faxed his work to his editor in Seattle, and he only wrote one page a day, in the morning, and every book he wrote was less than two hundred pages long. After he was done with his page he would eat a 24-ounce filet mignon steak and then pour a glass or rich amaretto over a pint of mint chocolate chip ice cream for dessert. Preceding dessert he would spend an hour coloring with large crayons on a fifty by twenty foot canvas. He would finish off one color each day on a small section of it. I finished the pad as room service was at my door. Timing, if there ever was such a thing, was always perfect when things were going to work out just right.

I tipped the guy at the door and charged the food to the room.

I ate and fell asleep. The phone rang. It felt as though I had just closed my eyes, but the clock read five hours later.

"Hello?" I said clearing my throat.

"Hank, darling, are you sleeping?" It was Juliet.

"Not anymore," I said.

"I'm at *The Palace.* You really must come here before you go back to Santa Monica tomorrow." She sounded drunk. "I have some friends here that I want you to meet. My friend Juliet, wait . . . I'm Juliet!" She laughed for a good minute about that. "I'll send a car for you."

"Don't bother."

"What?"

"I know where it is."

I really didn't care to go but I knew that if I fell back asleep I would wake up at four and be miserable by the time I saw Harriet.

I began walking to *The Palace* after I put on some fresh clothes and ran a comb through my hair. I had forgotten to brush my teeth. Whatever.

I looked at my watch. It didn't really matter what time it was, going somewhere I didn't want to be already made it too late. I suppose that was the same for a person who was *someone* they didn't want to be. Whatever.

Then, as I was walking, I remembered a dream I had while I was sleeping. It was a portrait of me sketching a sunset from a balcony with airplanes on the horizon.

I made it to the club.

It was a pretty garbage place, really. Probably full of every person that wanted to be a celebrity. Its face was a large and reflective silver, and there were red ropes leading the path to the doorway over a black carpet. I walked toward the doorway and could feel the bouncer eyeing me. Some punk kid, about twenty-two. He stopped me before the door.

"You can't go in. It's full," he said.

I looked at him, wanting to make a move, but declined.

"I'm meeting someone here."

"Right now, in there, everyone is meeting someone."

Smart-ass. I was going to walk away but Juliet hung over the balcony above and yelled for me to come up. Then she dropped a champagne flute, which broke on the black, carpeted walk. I went in.

The first floor of the club was sparsely filled and the only bartender had some girl's tongue in his ear so I decided to help myself. The bar was covered with cigarette ash and butts. I cleared them out of my way and just sat there at the bar with a tall glass of scotch enjoying the emptiness. I thought of how I was going back to the valley soon, and how I was going to see Harriet, too. Just then some girls stumbled through the doorway across from the bar, and I remembered that Juliet was expecting me. I looked at the glass of scotch, with air in half of it, and I looked at the bar all covered with cigarette ash and butts, and decided to walk back to the hotel. I could see Juliet the next day at the signing. Besides, the last thing I cared to see was some hundred pound girl with too much make-up on do a line of coke before jumping on some guy.

VIII

A chauffeured car drove me home the next morning. There was always a new driver wherever I went, and they always asked me the same questions. It grew to be very tiresome. When he dropped me home I dropped him a twenty-dollar bill and he put it in his pocket before looking at it, which is how I preferred the situation.

I walked to the grocery store and bought enough food for a few days. The phone rang while I was dusting out my cabinets. It was Robert Cambden.

"Hi Hank, how the hell are you?"

"You sound happy," I said.

"When old man Winters is happy, we're all happy. I have the week off and you to thank for it."

"Why is that?"

"The old man is very pleased with your current situation. In fact," he said, "he wants to sign you to another book."

"No shit? Funny thing is, I'm already into one. How did he hear about the reading so soon?"

"Reading? What . . . no. No one cares about that. He thinks you're going to marry Juliet."

"Why would he think that?"

"Well you're sleeping with her," he stated factually, "and Winters thinks you'll want to settle her down being that you're older and all."

"There's nothing between us."

44

"It's alright, listen I . . ."

"No, *you* listen, Robert. I would sooner scrub open sores on my body with lemons while chewing tin foil over a cavity-infected mouth."

"Look, it's alright. You writers always get so dramatic. We've all had our shots with her since she's been here. That's why she never finished a book. The old man wouldn't stand for it. But you lasted; you followed through. I mean, it's great having her around; she gives it up so easily. I haven't found the need for a new secretary in over a year."

"I'm going now," I said and hung up the phone.

I figured I would see Juliet's father at the signing, and I'd have to talk to him there. I finished putting away my groceries, mostly perishable goods.

The night wore on and as it approached ten o'clock I still hadn't called Harriet. I just sat down in my apartment and did nothing. I don't know why, but I did and I didn't see her that night. I unpacked my bag and finished *Timequake*, and then I fell asleep in my bed, feeling all out of place, but I fell asleep no less only to wake remembering no dreams I had the night before.

I took a long hot shower with soap and shampoo. Then I combed my hair and left for the bookstore, a mile from my apartment, with my copy of *The Woman's Suicide.*

It was a little store with a sign outside promoting a book signing by a local author. A few people were already waiting—a couple of unknowns trying to get out of jobs they hated. I tried to write something inspirational in poetic form. After all, I was collecting royalties. The least I could do is give them something they'd like.

The signing was scheduled from eleven to three. Harriet didn't show up. I was waiting for her to tell me how she missed me the night before and that I looked handsome, and then I would give her my copy of my book and she would read it.

Cambden showed up at the signing to see how it went. He didn't really care though. He only came by to tell me that no comments were made about my book by any of the critics. They didn't feel it was worth mentioning. Then, he left.

The book signing ended a little later than scheduled, and Mr. Winters showed up and stayed by my side until it was over.

"How is everything, Henri?" he asked. "Robert tells me you've gotten into a new book."

"Yes, I have."

"I trust all else is well. The reading went delightfully I was informed."

"How'd you hear that? I mean, there were no reviews."

"Juliet told me."

"Oh, yes. I see." I looked at my watch. "I'm sorry, Mr. Winters, but I must be off. I'll send you my second book as soon as I'm finished, but I'm afraid it will be my last."

"Why?"

"For now at least."

He looked confused.

"I was made an offer to work at a local college and, well, I don't believe in living to work so much as working to live."

"I see."

We shook hands and I exited the store. My throat was very dry. I had forgotten to eat before I left in the morning. I walked for a few blocks in no direction. I was glad for the silence and the sun that was hanging high in the sky. I was glad not to be trapped in a three-book deal. I didn't care what I was going to do. And although I knew that this reverted state would only have a short life I just enjoyed the mild humidity and the green leaves that were growing on the trees.

I continued to walk the sidewalks and I stopped at a market to buy some plums. As I walked out of the store I thought about the dream with the sunset and how I was sketching the airplanes on the horizon with all those colors. There was a dog barking at me while I was walking. He followed me for half a block or so. I didn't want him to get too close or my eyes would get puffy and irritated, so I crossed the street and entered the campus of the community college where some kids were standing on the corner speaking Spanish. It made me think of Harriet and the conversation we had on the phone while I was in LA; how she had had too much of me and said that it was over (she said it was over), and how even after an hour of weary talk it wasn't good enough (I wasn't good enough). It just wore her more and drove her further away.

I felt weak in my head and the plums fell from my hand. I stood there; hearing the Spanish-speaking kids on the corner while the sun stood over me, blazing on my temples and beating me down. And that was all that there was: the sun and the gravity, and the kids on the corner speaking Spanish while I was heaving over the bushes.

Timequake was due at the library, I had thought. I should return it before it's overdue. I tried to stand up straight, but my guts tugged at themselves and forced me over. I eventually fell and hit my head on the ground. I felt the little sticks from the bushes scratch against my face, and a big one went right into my chin. I wished it to my throat. No luck.

When I came to I was on a bed in the campus hospital. A nurse was stinging my face with rubbing alcohol. She said it was necessary. Pain is convenient, but never necessary. When she was done they took the i-v needle out of my arm and held some cotton over it to keep the blood in. They gave me my clothes and I dressed myself behind the curtain. Then I was taken to a desk where I was given a bill for $37.

"What's this for?" I asked.

"Your treatment. You can pay for it now or we can send the bill to you in the mail if you wish to pay later."

I told her to send it to me. She gave me a cup of water. The whole system sucked.

Thoughts of Harriet hit me as I stood there. She kept saying that I didn't care and that she didn't care for that. She kept saying that I stopped trying and that she was done trying too. She was so calm. She was always so calm, and she never showed herself to be too vulnerable or too human. She was evidently simple.

I walked out onto the street and the Spanish-speaking kids were still there. One of them had a shirt with a mailbox printed on it. They say it all starts and ends with the mailbox. I didn't own a mailbox.

IX

It was morning, the following day, and the weather was warm; very hot in fact. I looked over at my coffee table where loose-leaf pages from the night before were heaped in a scattered pile. I read them over and put them away. I scribbled an outline and some possible titles for the book. *The Finishing* seemed rather fitting, but it was just an idea, and not a very good one.

I stood up and was going to step into the shower for a few years, but then there was a knock at my door. It was the girl from the laundry corridor. I invited her in and began to feel sick. Her clothes were sticking to her body. She wanted to use my stove. Hers was out.

"Everything you'll need is underneath there, and there's some stuff in the refrigerator if you want," I told her.

"Okay," she said.

I left her there in the kitchen and grabbed the pages from the night before. I looked at myself in the mirror and wiped it clean with some tissue paper. Then I wiped the counter and the sink. I looked at the tub and cleaned it as well as the walls. I brushed my teeth and thought about shoving my toothbrush into my eyes with the bristle end, but I didn't. I turned the water on and let the tub fill half way but showering first felt preferable so I let the water down the drain and almost slipped as I stood up.

I leaned against the wall and replaced my feelings of weakness with thoughts of Harriet and how screwed up I was. I was just sitting there that night when I came home from LA, consciously unaware of what had happened, like some sort of an invalid. I washed my hair and my body, with an attempted reasoning, as the water went down the drain—she gave me what I wanted—and it all flowed counter-clockwise into the floor. I filled the tub and submerged myself over and over again. I think I was trying to drown myself, but I didn't. *God,* I thought, *how boring that is—suicide.* At least by living with myself I can suffer. Suffering is interesting, like an entire book. Suicide is more like a poem or the truth.

I stepped out of my tub feeling tired and hungry and weak. I dried off and put on the same clothes I wore the day before.

When I got out of the bathroom she was still there. I got a glass and filled it with milk, and sat down across from her. She thanked me. I told her not to mention it. We talked for a little while about the job she got fired from because she stopped giving the bosses *break benefits,* as they liked to call it. The supervisors would set up schedules of when they would give the girls their breaks, and two of the four girls would be *welcomed* to join them in the backroom for forty-five minutes off the clock. She said it wasn't worth barely making the rent. From the looks of her then it didn't look like she was making it at all, and I doubted that the landlord would have much trouble collecting some good faith payments until she could cover it with cash.

"How old are you?" I asked.

"How old are you?" she replied.

"Thirty-two."

"Okay," she said.

There was silence.

"Can you type?" I asked her.

"On a keyboard? Yeah."

50

"I have something I need done by the end of the week, but I have plans that are immovable. I'd be willing to pay you half now if you could do it for me."

She agreed. I gave her the pages and a roll of dimes to use the printer at the library.

"It's very important," I told her, "that this work is done by the end of the week. Here." I gave her the money and told her not to save the work on any discs, just to print it and give me the copies. She left.

I called Juliet. She was my only friend and I didn't like her. I wanted her to meet me for lunch; another potential whore that money I made might've been able to protect. She agreed and I brought the pad from my hotel.

We sat outside. It was crowded and the heat was so much that even she drank water with her bottle of new-century wine and her salad. We talked after we ate.

I told her a little about my childhood and she told me *all* about hers. Then she told me about when she went to Colorado State University and studied to be a teacher, but changed her mind when she found out that she had to go to graduate school and teach at the same time.

I gave her the pad from the hotel and asked her if she would type them for me. She put them in her bag.

I was still feeling tired. I wanted to sleep and the sun wasn't helping my condition. Juliet wanted to schedule four readings over the next month at poetry houses and another three signings at bookstores. I told her to do whatever. She didn't ask about the scratches on my face, and she wasn't so obvious either.

When I returned to my apartment it was getting dark and I saw the landlord exiting the girl's room. I realized that I still didn't know her name. He looked at me while he fastened his belt around his fat and blew a stream of smoke into the air from his cigar as he turned around, walking in the other direction. I suppose I figured it was too late because all I did was walk into my apartment and eat a banana that the heat fermented as I laid on the table in my kitchen and fell asleep waking to the sound of handwritten pages being shoved through my door slot . . . and the money with them.

I opened the door and looked both ways. No one was there.

The pages were in order and the money was all there, and I thought about when I first met her; how I thought it was amusing. I wasn't laughing then, at my door with the pages and the money. I don't think I've ever laughed in my whole life.

I finished the book once and was going to give it to Juliet so I could just get rid of it, but Harriet called me and wanted me to pick up my stuff from her place. I suggested somewhere for her to keep it, and she didn't like my suggestion, so we got into a fight. Well, I fought. She ended up dropping it in front of my door the next morning before she went to work before I was awake to see her. I wanted to see her.

I threw the book about the author aside. I began scribbling, and the scribbling continued for seven hours on a yellow note pad. When I reread it the next day it turned out to be a ten line poem, and I looked onward seeing a month of majesty before me. Terrible, terrible majesty. I wanted to die.

XI

I went to a car dealer and put a down payment on a Ford, mostly because I respected the assembly line. It gave a place to people without one. Very organized. Very simple.

I drove to San Deigo State and the University of San Francisco for readings and they paid me enough to get there and back, and eat along the way at decent restaurants. I didn't eat at decent restaurants. Readings are good for the long haul. You break even, which is good for the soul—for those with souls—on short terms. In the end it sells more books to students, and sometimes the institutions buy a couple of copies themselves.

The students are nice to read to. Most of them think they like poems and art, and the presence of an artist. The professors often spoke to me before it all started, and sometimes I got lucky and they didn't talk to me about art, but without that the only other thing they could relate me to was the traffic. That was okay, but not really, just better than the other. They didn't realize that I was no different, that I too got hungry at funerals, tucked my feet under the blankets at night, and emitted gallons of rectal gas over the course of a week.

The students, I found, wanted me to ask about *their* artistic license. They talked and were mostly very similar, but what the hell. They felt special and probably bought my book. It's money in my pocket for not really listening, because I heard it all before. Some people went to college

54

for ten years to do that. It all depended on how you played the game. I guess I got in a little late. Some never get in at all.

One young man was quite entertaining though. He had been writing poems for a little under a year, but it all started because a girl he wanted to have sex with, or something along those lines, was misinformed that he wrote poetry. He told her that he did. It turned out that she wrote as well and suggested that perhaps they could get together some time. He agreed and began writing so she wouldn't think he was a liar. To wrap it up—he went into great elaboration of how she went to study at a school in Phoenix—she liked his poems, but he hardly saw her. I usually found that poems alone are enough. And then he told me how he had forgotten to tell me that he told her the truth about how he came about his writing. She asked. Nobody likes to feel necessary, they just want to be told they are needed and left readily alone to their pointless little chores and contingencies. The truth doesn't make it too often. When it does, it is kept obscure or in a form of fairytale that none can relate to; only sit and watch.

In the middle of the month I was scheduled to read at *The Underground,* a poetry hole in LA. I showed up at seven. There were three other poets reading that night as well. I was scheduled to go on in an hour. Robert Prentice, a hundred-year-old author, was last to go on. It was said to be his last reading. He was ailing of colon cancer, and would be admitted into a hospital the next day. What a way to go, in some room that you've never been before; kept impersonal while the whole place is questionable.

The owner gave me fifty dollars and told me not to be up there for more than fifteen minutes. I think he was worried about Prentice making it.

At five to eight I got up on stage. It was odd. The stage was actually sunken and I sat in a chair raised nice and high. The table in front of me was old and clean and brown, and a microphone came through it. I adjusted it toward my face and pulled a poem out of the pile. It was thirty lines and people were walking in while I read so no one heard. They only wanted to see Prentice anyway. His was the only name on the list.

I could feel the cash through my pocket and kept reading. After my last poem some people clapped, then as I stood he came down the steps and sat at the bar. Everyone stood to applaud the old man. He was old, so old, and breathing. He was with a much younger woman. Her eyes were spirited, her body was natural, and she looked like my mother. Prentice walked up to the stage and organized his many published books. The owner paid the other poets to leave.

Prentice left his books on the table and asked for a bottle of Cognac. He did not appreciate the brand and would not read without it. He sat next to me at the table.

"So, Frenchman, what do you have?" he asked.

"Just water."

He gave me an unpleasing look of dissatisfaction.

"Don't let them do it to you," he said, "you're not a kid anymore, and you've paid your dues. Don't let the teachers tell you different."

"What's your brand?" I asked, referring to the Cognac he wanted.

"Louis XIV. He won't bring it back, not from a place around here."

I drank my water.

"Here," he said, "get used to this. It tastes just awful, but no worse than anything else you're going to swallow."

He took my glass and threw the water and the ice on

the floor and filled it a little over half. He filled his glass a half inch at a time and drank it slowly.

"That's pretty disgusting," I told him.

"Get used to it."

We sat drinking the Cognac, and he introduced me to his daughter, Matilda, who looked like my mother. She was about sixty years old and didn't say anything. She just drank her drink and sat very intently while her father told me what it was like being an expatriate, how the socialites resented him for being a young writer, like them, and how he resented them as he got more and more money, so he gave it away.

"You have to be smarter than I, Henri. Be smarter than I," he said. "They won't praise credit to you until you're dead when they can keep it all for themselves."

"I'm sorry, Robert."

"Sorry?"

"For your dying and not knowing it then."

"Com'ere kid," he said. I leaned over and his eyes met mine as he spoke again. "I figured they'd accept it if I died of the shits, but dysentery is rather confining. Take a plague and never die. It's not the only way for us, but it can do you very well. Look around," he said, "just look."

I looked and saw the people sitting at their smoke-free tables, but all I could see was an audience and fifty dollars in my pocket.

Then the owner came in and placed a box on the table, opened it, and there was a bottle of Louis XIV resting upon a blanket of velvet.

Prentice smiled heartily pleased and approached the stage. It was eleven o'clock by then and every table had extra chairs beside them. He took a pen and wrote on the inside cover of all his books, thanked the crowd for being there and auctioned off his autograph. Someone paid $8,000 for the last one. The binding it was attached to went for $17.95 retail.

Matilda then went up to the stage and handed him a piece of paper. He recited the words from it, which ended in a wild, gracious applause. He thanked them and walked toward the door. As he walked out with his daughter the crowd silenced. He turned to them and said, "dogs are rumored to be more loyal," and exited the establishment.

I saw the bottle of Louis XIV on stage. I picked it up and ran out into the streets to retrieve him. I saw Matilda on a corner across the street. She was standing over Robert who was on the ground. I picked him up slowly. He fell on the cheap bottle of Cognac and the glass was in his wrist. I brought him to my car and he pulled out a shard, which allowed for the removal of much blood.

"It was so easy," he said. Then he laid his head back slowly.

I started the car and drove to the hospital. He was unconscious after several minutes. He was probably dead as I carried him into the emergency entrance. I didn't know where Matilda was.

Robert Prentice, an American expatriate and the most self-allowed author (and I mean real authors, not writers) that ever lived was pronounced dead on August 17 of abrasions to the wrists. The newspapers were very vague, and the public held great appreciation for his passing.

He chose a plague but died as a child could have. He died as a loser or a madman could have. They wrote about him in the papers, and a tabloid printed my picture next to his headlining, **Driven by the Madness.** He died as a child could have.

XII

The funeral was held three days later. I made all the arrangements. The expenses were covered by the money Prentice made auctioning off his books. He was buried in a large shiny coffin and a three-piece suit. I filled a flask with six ounces of Louis XIV and placed it in the left inside pocket of his coat.

I didn't feel very good about burying him in California, but I didn't know where Matilda was, and I didn't want to let the old man's body rot, though I suppose it did anyway.

It was very hot the day he was buried. I bought a suit and wore it—black. The priest continued endlessly, and even the reporters grew tired. Eventually we all lowered our heads in prayer as the casket was lowered into the ground, and the photographers snapped their cameras a few times as I wiped the sweat from my brows and my lips. Matilda was across the grave, looking at me. I didn't notice her before. She looked at me very solemnly and raised her left forefinger to her eye, let it slide down her cheek, then her right, and let it slide down her cheek. She stepped into the grave but no one noticed. They were all talking or leaving with their cameras, and I ran to the grave and almost fell in myself. A few snapping sounds were made. No one was in there, just the coffin.

"Mr. Manson . . ." I heard a voice, "Mr. Manson."

"What?" I turned my head, and looked toward the grave. There was nothing there, just a hole in which the coffin lay. I was out for a little while, or, at least, it didn't seem very long.

"Are you alright?"

"Yes. Yes. Who are you?"

She was a photographer for the *Chicago Times*. Her skin was fair and she was short. Her name was Harriet. She spoke with me for several minutes and asked if I was available to go to dinner with her. I told her I didn't like her face, that her hair needed trimming at the ends, and that it was her forehead that disgusted me most, but if she didn't have the forehead it would have been her nose that was too high above her gangly lips and spread her eyes too far apart, and that if she ever thought about killing herself she should get to it as soon as possible so that there could be another seat open for a standby passenger on the flight that would have departed here, and her life could have had some purpose.

I walked over to his grave again, looked down, and only saw a box. I shoveled some dirt into the hole and wiped the sweat from my face as I passed by the girl again, and removed my coat. I drove away feeling very tired and very blank. My car needed gas.

I pulled into a gas station and filled the tank half way with regular, paid, and left. I drove away thinking, *I don't think I've ever seen a parent yell at their kids in a gas station,* as the fumes remained quite salient. When I returned to my apartment I laid on my couch and ate a bowl of grapes while looking at the ceiling, and I fell asleep and had a dream that I was driving a delivery truck down an empty road but there was nothing to deliver. I pulled up to a yellow light turned red . . .

. . . and woke up at nine o'clock at night, rushed out the door and drove around the city feeling very aware of my face. I wanted to take a shower, or, at least splash some water on myself. I was very thirsty, and very sober. I ended up in a bar in LA that some movie star owned where they wouldn't serve me alcohol but I could have all the air I wanted. Club Oxygen. The place was packed and everyone touched each other, and I couldn't leave. I drank five Charmonies and soon enough I was sitting in the back room with some photographer from Chicago with short legs and a small frame breathing oxygen from large tanks. I felt like I was flying.

In the morning I woke up in a strange room in my apartment alone on a wet spot on my bed. I remembered laughing and feeling very high, and then we started and I ended and then we started again and again, and I ended again and again. We both looked down each time and laughed a lot. She stopped laughing shortly after the third one and I fell asleep after she left, and there was no more reason to laugh, and I found myself grounded with the same question running continuously through my mind as I asked myself, *How the hell did I get here?*

XIII

Some time went by. I was all over the newspapers because of the constant reporting of Prentice. Reporters called me asking for interviews and pictures, and I told them no but that didn't matter. Eventually they found out where I lived so I just stepped outside and let them take all the pictures they wanted. They wanted me to get angry (I could tell by their questions) but they eventually ran out of film, and all they got was a smile along with some clever poses. None of them were printed—I guess they were waiting for me to die.

I was reading frequently. The money was starting to be a hassle so I put it into a checking account. The larger bookstores asked me to come in for signings, and I was even invited back to San Diego State University to speak to their incoming freshman class, but I turned it down because of the short notice.

I was starting to think I was breaking even after all those years, but I didn't feel differently about anything. My television was still a picture of snow, and my mattress needed new springs, but I was eating more and writing better, less, but better. I usually found that that was how the whole thing worked. I thought about joining a gym. I thought about buying a new desk, and maybe some fountain pens.

I didn't do any of those things.

Two weeks after the funeral I was driving down the

street. It was still very hot out and some of the stores were selling air conditioners on clearance. I stopped at a red light and I heard someone on the street say, "Isn't that the guy that killed Prentice?" I looked over and saw three kids, about fourteen. I looked forward. *What the hell do they know?* I thought to myself. And as the light turned green I took one last glance only to see them mooning me. I rather appreciated that. I only wish I'd had a camera.

Anyhow, I screamed out of my window for them to pick up their pants because someone might get the wrong idea, and someone took a picture of me screaming out of the window of my car and it was printed in the traffic section of the newspaper. It seemed that everyone was in on the feast.

For the next two weeks I stayed in my apartment with the exception of the few readings I didn't cancel. I just wrote at my kitchen table, had my groceries delivered, and even took up painting. The painting wasn't very good but it helped me pass the time. It was better than the modern stuff, but what wasn't? Modern poetry, modern art, dancing to modern music. All you had to do was throw everything all over the place and people called you an expert because they hardly ever looked at the stuff, and, as sad as it may be [it's not that sad] they couldn't do it themselves. I felt like I was the only one that had a problem with it. Whatever. Maybe I was.

Toward the end of September I received a bank statement. $857.16 (there was more than that though). It was a satisfying sight. I had just finished my second novel and a book of poems called *The Wayward Signs,* and there was money in the bank. I went to call Juliet, but dialed Harriet's phone number by mistake. A man answered.

"Hullo," he said clearing his throat.

"Hello."

"Yes?" he asked.

"Sorry, I must've dialed . . . "

"Who is it?" a voice in the background asked. It was Harriet. "No one," he replied, and hung up the phone. I hung up as well and dialed right the second time. Maybe I deserved that. I told Juliet that I was coming by to drop off the books.

When I arrived she wasn't in her office so I waited close to an hour for her. When she came in I think she was startled that I was there.

"Oh. Hi."

"I just thought I'd wait for you. I'm leaving tomorrow and was wondering if you wanted to come with me."

"Where are you going?"

"Las Vegas. I've never been, and thought it would be fun. So what d'ya say?"

"No. I really can't. Thanks, though."

We spoke for a few more minutes and she was indifferent. I left it at that, and I was pissed off because if I had had sex with her two months before she probably would've taken me herself. I went to the bank before it closed and withdrew $600. I had another $300 at my apartment. I threw a pair of pants and two shirts in a bag. I had forgotten socks and underwear. I was rushing. On my way out I managed to grab some food so I wouldn't have to stop along the way. I did, for gas, but that was all.

When I arrived it was still bright out, but very dry. The streets seemed to be getting busier, and the prostitutes were difficult to make out. I drove into a casino parking lot and took my ticket. There was a convention of some sort that was leaving as I was walking in. The cheapest room was $98. I don't know where they got their prices, but I paid for a night. When I got to my room there was just a bed, a bathroom, and a T.V. I laid on the bed and scared the crap out of myself as I looked up and saw my reflection on the ceiling. *What a dumb idea,* I thought.

After a few hours of sleep I got up and realized that I forgot to bring a toothbrush and a razor. The hotel store had them but I just pissed in the shower and washed my face and my hair. Then I went to one of the restaurants near the casino where I ate about $3 worth of food at the $15 buffet.

I walked around on the street for a while. I didn't care for it. You see, Las Vegas is apparently a great family place, which is very obvious by all of the old men walking around with their *daughters.* Eventually I just went back to the hotel casino and sat down at a $15 blackjack table. I wasn't so bad actually. I got blackjack on my first two hands and the people playing against the dealer felt good about it too. A waitress came around and I asked for a cognac, but she didn't get it back to me for fifteen minutes and by that time I was down $75. *What the hell,* I thought, *I came here a loser anyway.* I gave the waitress $20 and asked her to bring me another, but a little more quickly. A woman sitting next to me in a nice dress ordered the same. She was just about even, but not quite. See, blackjack pays 3:2, and it seemed that she would get blackjack once in a while, but lose the next two hands. Other than that she would routinely win and then lose, and then win again and lose again until she eventually hit blackjack. They don't have decks of cards either. The dealers dealt from a chute of ten or twelve decks, and they were both rotated often. The cognacs came and I was even again, but I felt like I was winning. The woman and I got to talking. She seemed interested and I felt like a loser so it was nice. She was a working girl. I shouldn't have been surprised but I just wasn't thinking.

By midnight I still had some chips left and I was only down $15. At the end of the third chute of cards I had almost lost $300, but the next one was very good to me. Charlotte, the woman next to me, didn't have as much luck as the cards kept coming out. We were still talking and it just would have been a waste of her time to have had three cognacs and all that conversation with nothing to show for it, so I told her I'd like to spend the night with her, but I wanted her to buy my book. She wanted $1,000. I didn't have that much money, but for what I did have she would give me an hour or two depending on how long I lasted.

"You don't have to be there in the morning," I told her. "You can leave as soon as I fall asleep."

She agreed for $500, but she wasn't going to buy my book.

We went back to my room and she took off her dress, and then her shoes. She was a white woman with brown hair and blue eyes, about 5'6". She asked me what I wanted and I told her to lay down. She did, and I massaged her calves for a few minutes, then her shoulders until she fell asleep. It was a dirty trick, I suppose, but we wanted different things. I just decided that I wanted to win that night.

I put the covers over her and stared out at the lights of the city. They shone over her and I could see her rounded shoulder and her neck as her head rested upon the pillow. She breathed very lightly and I slipped under the blanket alongside of her after putting my watch in my pocket and getting undressed.

How clever: a watch in the pocket.

Eventually I fell asleep for a few hours, but only a few hours. I think I just wanted to watch her sleep. At six o'clock I rolled over and put my arm around her. It woke her up and she sat up immediately, looked outside, and got out of bed.

She looked at the clock, then at me, and walked into the bathroom with her purse. I could hear the shower running. She dried her hair and I walked out of the room with her to see her to the front door of the hotel while no words were exchanged. I watched her walk east for about half a block. I went back to the room, put the complimentary soaps in my bag, had breakfast at the other restaurant next to the casino, and left after paying for my car's time in the parking lot. I didn't see Wayne Newton or the showgirls, but I felt pretty bad, so there was that.

The phone was ringing as I walked into my apartment. It was a reporter/writer from *The New Yorker*. It seemed that *Time* magazine was going to run an article called "Driven by the Madness" about Prentice and me. He wanted me to write my own account of that night with Prentice.

"So, what do you say?" he asked.

I told him I wasn't interested.

"Can I at least interview you so *I* can accurately write about it?"

"No."

"I can do it over the phone. If it's about the money . . . "

I hung up the phone.

It rang. I picked it up. Same guy again. I hung up the phone and let it ring until I disconnected it rather than rip it out of the wall like I wanted to. He wasn't worth a new phone. I just sat down at my table after punching the wall, but not very hard, and read my mail.

I received credit card information, a bill for a car payment, and an invitation to appear at a convention held by the Seattle City Council on the first weekend of November. I thought that it was a little short of notice given the event, but I called to accept and they said they'd pay for me to fly there first class, and pay me $1,000. They also added that some pictures would be taken with the mayor. I figured that by then all of the excitement would have settled, and that I would be dead to the world, as I preferred.

XIV

I believe it was October, but it felt like April. I thought about April . . . the April before that one. In a year and a half; from no thoughts or cares or hope; from a life absent of all but guilt and blame, lacking pity, I felt wealthy. I could have used some new sheets, and perhaps some towels, but I felt wealthy. I constantly thought about suicide and craft and form. I wasn't always like that. All I ever thought about then was living long enough to forget everything that had ever happened, since I knew that forgiveness was impossible. There was nothing to forgive. There was no reason. I didn't do anything and negligence is a crime of many forms.

I bought a new couch that didn't seem to fit my apartment so I cleaned my apartment. I figured out how much money it would take to replace all of my stuff and move into a nicer place. It came out to be a little more than I would have had after the convention in Seattle, excluding the moving fee. I suddenly needed movers. Prentice would have taken care of the whole thing had I spoken to enough reporters, but he had already paid enough. His time was done.

It was Tuesday and I was sleeping. The phone woke me up. It was Cambden, I thought. He asked me to meet him for lunch. I *thought* it was Cambden.

I laid back in bed and almost fell back into my sleep,

but didn't. I got out of bed, wiped my hands over my face and took a pair of underwear, pants, and an undershirt into the bathroom. I couldn't find my bathrobe. I might have thrown it out. I brushed my teeth, shaved, and stepped into the shower. It was noon, but I didn't know that. I dried off and put my clothes on. Then I brushed my hair after putting on a new shirt, and I drove to a deli where Harriet was waiting for me. It was she who called. Why did I think it was Cambden?

"Hi," she said. She stood up and kissed my cheek, but didn't really kiss my cheek.

"Hi." I felt awkward. "I'm going to get something."

I went over to the refrigerator and pulled out a quart size bottle of pineapple juice and got a paper coffee cup. I sat down across from her after paying.

"Pineapple juice?"

"I know. Grapefruit juice is better, but it's too much for me."

She looked at me as though she'd never met me before.

"Why is your hair straight?" I asked.

We sat and talked about nothing at all for five, maybe ten, minutes. She liked her new students for the most part. One of them tried to push himself on her, but she took care of that with a thumb to his solar plexus. That usually happened once a year. I told her that I was reading regularly, and that I bought a new car, went north for a little while, then south, and took a drive out of state. She said that she was looking forward to reading my book, that she was pretty busy for a while but wanted to get to it. She seemed pleased that two more books were coming out, and she said that she was happy that I was doing so well.

Eventually I talked to her about Prentice; what had happened that night. I told her all of the things he told me, how I carried him into the hospital dead—the bloodstains

69

that were still in my car. I told her about the papers, but she already knew that. I told her about the public, but she already knew that too. I felt very obvious and vulnerable. I guess I meant to be obvious. She was wearing a white shirt and gray pants. Her hair was longer and her face was thinner. She was doing very well without me.

I thought about apologizing for the fight I had with her the last time we spoke, but didn't.

"Are you seeing anyone?" I asked.

"No," she said. "I was, but not anymore."

"Who was he?"

"A teacher." She wasn't looking at me anymore.

"If you don't want to talk about it . . ."

"It's alright."

"I mean with me."

We didn't talk about the relationship. He was forty and taught psychology at the city college. He was probably a good guy, but what was she going to do with a rebound? On our way out I bought some cold cuts and three fresh rolls. I walked her to her car, and we both looked at each other and smiled uncomfortably. I wanted to kiss her mouth. She might have let me, but I didn't. We shook hands and gave each other a friendly kiss goodbye, and I went back to my apartment with the feel of her lips on mine. I began to masturbate but stopped after fifteen minutes. What was the point? I only would have felt worse afterward. I fell asleep on my couch in front of my television and dreamt that I was on a block in suburbia with nice houses down the entire road. It seemed to go on for as far as I could see.

There was a little girl there, too, and she was speaking to me. I was very uncomfortable around her, almost frightened. 'He shouldn't have done it,' she said, 'I told him not to,' 'I know you did. Everything's going to be alright. Things have a way of working out,' I told her. She wasn't convinced. 'It was wrong anyway.' 'I know,' I said. 'No. It rained and now his shoes are all wet.' 'He didn't know it was going to rain. How could he have known that?' She looked at me and walked away. I didn't follow her, or move at all. She returned shortly and opened her mouth to speak, but all there was, was static. I thought about my T.V. It was still on. I tried to focus on her—on my dream—but I was too aware of it all so I got off of my couch and turned it off. It was almost midnight. My sleeping pattern was off again, and I had two weeks of readings scheduled before I would be in Seattle.

XV

I feel like I've told this part before. The readings paid for the bed I slept in, which was reason enough for me to show up. I found that most places I read at already had a dozen or so copies of *The Woman's Suicide* for sale. It was nice to see.

Some of the women would have liked it if I had taken them home, but what was I going to do with them? Some of the men would have liked that, too, but that was more of a question of what they may have wanted to do with me. I often found myself in the same place after reading. I would go back to my apartment with an inability to write anything good, so I would paint something bad. There was no balance between my writing and my reading, and too much of one killed the other while the other fed the killer. It didn't really matter though. The book of poems was going to be released in late November and the novel about the author would be all ready in March. I figured that the press gave me a year to do nothing but collect. I just had to make sure I didn't get too lazy because it beat the hell out of working in a cannery, or some crummy store, or some other place I'd read about some other guy working in.

I always found some trouble with acquiring menial jobs that required little thought. I think part of it was that I didn't look dumb, and although I wasn't that tall I looked even smaller than I was, so labor jobs were out.

I tried to get a job in a lumberyard once. The boss was

about my size but fatter, and he sat behind his desk looking at my job application, which took me an hour to fill out. I wanted it to look neat. I don't think that helped.

"What are you," he asked me, "about five-six? Five-seven?"

"Five-nine."

I don't think he wanted to believe me.

"You're about a buck and a quarter?"

"One-fifty."

"I see some college here. Why do you want this job?"

I told him I had this habit of eating once in a while.

"Well," he said, "I understand it's tough, but we are facing a recession . . ." he went on for a little but I think you see how it went. Most places just told me that they weren't hiring, or that they wanted someone with experience.

Juliet stopped showing up to the readings, and we hadn't spoken to each other since I went to Vegas. She was probably too busy giving Cambden hand jobs while he talked to her father on the phone. Whatever. It was her life. Besides, if it weren't for Cambden I'd still have been in that moldy sub-ground office, sucking in fifty-year-old dust with the bugs and my scotch. It was just part of the trade-off. We have to bargain it all away eventually; some just don't get to be there to watch it happen.

It was a Tuesday, Halloween I believe, when she had finally decided to call me. She was on her way out to a party, and I think she was hoping to leave a message on my machine. She asked about the readings and I asked why she really called. She wasn't going to Seattle with me for the convention. I told her that it was fine and we hung up the phone. I drank a glass of water, ate some olives—black—and fell asleep with the lights on.

I woke up at four in the morning with no memories of any dreams.

I took my ten canvasses into the middle of the grass in front of my apartment, threw a little turpentine on the top one, and watched it burn. I realized how pointless that was—the drama, I mean—as I walked back into my apartment and threw my paints and brushes in the garbage, keeping the smock and the turpentine.

At seven o'clock I called Harriet and asked her if she would come with me to Seattle. She said no. I think she was being smart. She usually was.

XVI

Harriet died.

She died on a Thursday—the next day. I received a phone call from the college at three, but I was at a store buying a coat and a suitcase. She could have used me as a donor and they could have completed a transfusion at the college medical center, but by the time I returned the call she was at another one. No one in her family could be reached and she died on the way over because there wasn't a single pint of type A positive blood. When I finally arrived all I could do was identify her body, but that was already taken care of.

She looked pale. I didn't want to see her like that. She was just a rested cold mass that never had to love or hate or think ever again. She was new. She got to start over.

The hospital spent the next twenty-four hours looking for her family. I knew she had some family. I met her brother and her mother once. They were nice but the hospital couldn't find them. I started making plans to put her in the ground. Her insurance wouldn't cover any of it, and her school said that since she wasn't actually a member of the faculty she could only receive a limited amount of money, and that it could only be collected by her immediate family.

Everything was arranged for Saturday. She was put

into an oversized wooden casket and she wore a nice dress. They put flowers in her hands. It didn't even look like her.

Thirty people were there; some of them were reporters. I wanted to grieve, but they wouldn't let it happen shamelessly. They all had their cameras ready and right up in my face; it made me want to scream because all I wanted to do was cry.

The pastor delivered his sermon and the casket was lowered into the ground. It ended and everyone left. I stood there for some moments but they wouldn't cover her until nightfall. I wanted to join her, but knew that I never could.

"Hank." It was Cambden. He and Juliet attended the service. They helped me find a proper cemetery along with most of everything else.

"Let us leave him alone, Robert. Hank," Juliet said, "we'll be by the car. Take your time." She squeezed my hand. "I'm sorry." She said she was sorry, and then she went away.

It was late morning. The sky was there and the grass was there, hanging over and under the endless yard of tombstones. And below all of that were all of the empty boxes with their weight to hold them down. I looked at her plot. I wanted to sit. There was a heavy lump in my throat and my head hurt. My stomach felt heavy and empty.

"So this is how it ends? You didn't even say goodbye this time." I stood there and thought about the way she laughed. I had it on a loop in my mind. I remembered her looks; when she looked as though she had never met me when we were in the deli, the times that I was drunk or drinking. She only laughed once that I ever heard, but it had been so long ago that it was no longer real. She liked to laugh. Most people don't, but she did. She liked to make love, too, I remembered. She was into fairness and justice, and people who worked hard the right way, but all of that came to me then during the moments before the sight of her empty coffin; not when it mattered between her and me. Sometimes I think that if I had a better relationship with God that I could have felt more justified by my dilatory recollections, but I didn't, so I didn't. It didn't mean anything anyway.

"I'm going to, um . . . well, I'm going to say goodbye now."

I stood there. The clouds came over a little and I walked away from the sky and the grass and the coffin. Cambden opened the door for me, and Juliet sat in the back seat. I blew my nose into a handkerchief and wiped my eyes with another.

Cambden drove out of the cemetery and to a restaurant. We took a table outside. The street was clear of traffic but it wasn't a very busy street anyway. The restaurant was almost full inside. I sat with my back to the street and Cambden sat to my right.

The waiter came over. Juliet ordered a plate of fruit and a side of rye toast. Cambden insisted that I order next. I asked for a cup of coffee. Cambden got a bagel, and a glass of orange juice, and a cup of coffee.

The waiter brought us our coffees right away and spilled some into the little plate underneath my cup. As I stirred some sugar into it a young man approached me and asked if I was responsible for the book he was holding. I told him that I was and he asked me to sign it for him. I did. I looked at him and he was staring at me with ocean-blue eyes that were shot red where all the white should've been. He asked me if I ever wrote anything under the name of Jonathan Henri. I told him I didn't. He remained until I turned around to face Cambden and Juliet; my only friends, and Cambden and I drank our bloody coffees, and I wanted to look at the sun long enough so that I would never see anything ever again, but didn't.

We all just sat there and no one said anything. Inside the restaurant I saw them drinking their bloody coffees and eating their crummy pastries while the sun burned my skin, and my hair felt hot. The weather was predicted to rain. It didn't look like rain.